ALONE TOGETHER

ON
DAN STREET

By Erica Lyons
Illustrated by Jen Jamieson

APPLES & HONEY PRESS

Apples & Honey Press
An Imprint of Behrman House Publishers
Millburn, New Jersey 07041
www.applesandhoneypress.com

ISBN 978-1-68115-596-8

Text copyright © 2022 by Erica Lyons
Illustrations copyright © 2022 by Behrman House

Library of Congress Cataloging-in-Publication Data

Names: Lyons, Erica, author. | Jamieson, Jen (Illustrator), illustrator.
Title: Alone together on Dan Street / by Erica Lyons ; illustrated by Jen Jamieson.
Description: Millburn, New Jersey : Apples & Honey Press, [2022] | Audience: Grades K-1 | Summary: "A young girl practices the Four Questions on her apartment balcony in Jerusalem, and finds a way to bring the neighbors together for Passover even during the separation of a pandemic"-- Provided by publisher.
Identifiers: LCCN 2021035881 | ISBN 9781681155968 (hardcover)
Subjects: CYAC: Jews--Fiction. | Epidemics--Fiction. | Neighbors--Fiction. | Jerusalem--Fiction.
Classification: LCC PZ7.1.L965 Al 2022 | DDC [E]--dc23
LC record available at https://lccn.loc.gov/2021035881

Design by Alexandra N. Segal
Edited by Dena Neusner
Printed in China

9 8 7 6 5 4 3 2 1

It was the year the singing stopped.

The streets across Jerusalem were silent.

The Western Wall plaza was empty.

The shops on Jaffa Road were shuttered.

To stay safe from a bad virus,
everyone stayed home.
School closed and
synagogue was canceled too.

Playdates ended.
Purim was barely there.

Passover,
Mira
thought,
would
be
different
too.

Everyone was home, all day every day.
Still, Ima and Abba, working in robes and slippers,
baked warm cookies with Mira and her brother, Zach.

They had family game nights and read
her favorite storybooks.

Mira missed the park, the playground, and dance class. But she missed art class on Wednesdays most of all.

Now the days were all mixed up, and sometimes
the nights too. And seasons were only things that
happened on the balcony. Every picture she drew
was of the same building across the street.

She memorized the shape of each golden-hued
brick of Jerusalem stone. She knew where the
stray tabby cat liked to sleep and that the
purple flowers were about to bloom.

Then one day, Abba announced that it was almost Passover.

Mira wondered how so much time had passed outside while they were inside.

THE FOUR QUESTIONS

TOYS

"It's time to start practicing the Four Questions for the seder," Ima said.

"What seder?" Mira asked.
"I thought no one can come over this year!"

"You're still the youngest in the house, and guests or no guests, we will celebrate."

Mira tried to practice, but Abba
was always on Zoom in the living room.
Ima was always on the phone in the kitchen.

Zach was always studying in their bedroom.

So she went to the only place
she could be alone,

the balcony.

"Mah nishtanah, ha-lailah ha-zeh . . .
Why is tonight different . . ." she sang out
to the empty street.

"*. . . mi-kol ha-leilot? . . .* from all other nights?"
sang Mr. Blum from the next-door balcony,
taking Mira's next line.

This made her giggle.

"Something funny, Mira?"
Mr. Blum asked.

Mr. Blum always said funny things,
like "I'm not getting *a* haircut,
I'm getting them *all* cut."

"The Four Questions is the part for the
youngest person in the house to sing.
You're not young. You're a grandpa," Mira said.

"True, but I'm the youngest in my house this year. I'm also the oldest. Because of the virus, I'm all alone for the holiday."

"Then we can practice together," Mira suggested.
"I would like that very much," Mr. Blum said.

The Four Questions

Why is this night different
from all other nights?

On all other nights, we eat bread or matzah.
Why do we eat only matzah tonight?

On all other nights, we eat all kinds of
herbs. Why do we eat only bitter
herbs tonight?

On all other nights, we do not dip herbs
even once. Why do we dip herbs
twice tonight?

On all other nights, we eat either sitting
or reclining. Why do we recline tonight?

And so they did.

Mah Nishtanah

Mah nishtanah halailah hazeh mikol haleilot?

Sheb'chol haleilot anu och'lin chameitz umatzah. Halailah hazeh kulo matzah.

Sheb'chol haleilot anu och'lin sh'ar y'rakot. Halailah hazeh maror.

Sheb'chol haleilot ein anu matbilin afilu pa'am echat. Halailah hazeh, sh'tei f'amim.

Sheb'chol haleilot anu och'lin bein yoshvin uvein m'subin. Halailah hazeh kulanu m'subin.

Every afternoon, from their balconies, Mira and Mr. Blum sang together.

But as Passover got closer, Mira thought more about what it meant for Mr. Blum to be without his family for the seder. Passover was about welcoming strangers.

"Let those who are hungry come and eat," they said every year. How could Mr. Blum be alone?

And it wasn't just Mr. Blum.

There was Mrs. Yaso
on the second floor.
Mrs. Cohen on the third.
Mr. Penkar on the fourth.

They all lived alone —
and that was just the
people in her building.

What about the rest
of the neighborhood?

With markers, paints, and colored paper, Mira now had something special to create.

She drew pictures of the people she saw from her balcony and made them into beautiful invitations for all of Dan Street.

"Let's sing together at our balcony seders."

The next day, she passed the invitations across to
Mr. Blum, along with Passover macaroons.

He passed the
invitations up
to Mrs. Yaso,
along with a
basket of fruit.

She passed them on to Mrs. Cohen, with a pot of stew, who passed them to Mr. Penkar, with a brisket.

Soon there were colorful invitations and tasty treats up and down Dan Street.

When the first night of Passover came, Mira took the seder plate off the dining room table and carried it to the balcony.

"Mira, where are you going with that? We're ready to start," Ima cried.

"Just wait," Mira said.

At that exact moment, all of Dan Street started to sing the first words of the seder.

And it wasn't just Dan Street.

From all over the neighborhood, small voices and large voices, old voices and young voices rang out from balconies and windows.

And when Mira sang the Four Questions,
she was joined by a choir larger and
happier than she could have imagined.

It was the year of singing
with one another.

No one was together,
but no one was alone.

A Note to Families

This tale is based on the true story of a time when people had to stay inside and away from each other to protect themselves from the coronavirus, a very contagious disease. In Jerusalem, Israel, where Mira lives, many people actually did move their Passover seders onto their balconies, so that no one would feel alone.

Sometimes when people are alone, they also feel lonely. Have you ever felt lonely? What helps you feel better when you are lonely? When someone else feels lonely, what can you do to try to help them?

Coming together as a community, as Mira and her neighbors did on their balconies, can show us that we are not truly alone because we are surrounded by people who care.